The Real McCoy

Susan McCloskey
Illustrated by Charles Shaw

Rigby

Contents

1

The Mean Kid

The first time Devin saw the mean kid was the morning after he and his mom arrived in Maine. Mom had walked Devin to the pier and left to go to the diner that his grandmother owned. Devin looked for a good place to fish. He found one next to a thick piling.

Devin sat down and baited his hook with a raw clam. Then he dropped his line into the sea and leaned against the piling. He sat there comfortably in the warm sun, lost in thought as he watched the ferry to the islands steam by. Just then an unfriendly voice above him made him jump.

"You're in my fishing spot," the voice said. Devin looked up and saw a dark-haired boy standing over him. The boy had a fierce look. Without a word, Devin reeled in his line, got up, picked up his pail of bait and his tackle box, and went home.

He told his grandmother about the boy. "He wasn't trying to be mean," Gram said. "That's how it

1

is around here. You're the new kid in town. That boy
has probably lived here all his life. Maybe he's had that
spot ever since he was big enough to hold a fishing
pole. Maybe his dad fished there before him. And his
granddad before that. Don't let it bother you. Just find
a different spot. Use it all the time, and it'll get to be
your fishing spot."

So Devin found a different spot, as far away from
the dark-haired boy as he could get. They sometimes
crossed each other's paths, though. Devin would see
him at the bait shack or walking on the pier. But they
would always pass each other with their heads down,
not speaking. Devin always looked at the boy out of
the corner of his eye, taking in every detail of the boy's
face, especially the thick eyebrows, the strong chin,
and the look that said, "I dare you to speak to me!"
And Devin wasn't very daring. That was one of his
big problems.

It didn't help any that, as Devin's grandmother
said, he was the new kid in town. The town was Blue
Harbor, Maine. Devin and his mom had just arrived
there from New York City.

Devin's parents let him decide if he wanted to
spend the summer in Maine with his mom and
grandmother or stay in New York with his dad and

older brother. Devin didn't have to come, and his experience with the unfriendly kid made him wonder if he had made a big mistake..

2

The Decision

It all begin one June evening a few weeks earlier. The family—Mom, Dad, Devin, and Devin's older brother John—were playing a noisy word game in their small apartment in New York City. Devin had just picked one of the word cards from the box in the middle of the table. "Heat lamp," he read to himself before passing the card to John. A pleasant panic filled him. How on earth was he going to draw a picture of a heat lamp?

"Ready?" Dad asked. Then he turned over the hourglass timer, and Devin and John began drawing.

"Candle? Fireplace? Radiator?" guessed Mom. With each guess Devin shook his head and kept drawing. Mom's guesses got crazier and crazier. Devin was laughing so hard that he could hardly hold the pencil.

From what he heard of Dad's guesses, John's pictures weren't any better than his.

Just then the phone rang.

"The McCoy residence," Mom answered. "This is the real McCoy speaking." Everyone in the family answered the phone that way.

Mom's joking tone quickly turned serious.

"You *what?* Are you okay?" By now the hourglass timer had run out, and no one was paying any attention to the game. All eyes were on Mom. She glanced at Dad. "It's Gram," she silently mouthed to him.

Gram was Mom's mother. She lived in Blue Harbor, where she ran a diner called Gram's. Gram and Gramps had owned the diner together, but he had died five years earlier. Now Gram was on her own.

Gram and Mom talked for a while. After they hung up, Mom said, "Gram fell and broke her ankle. It's in a cast. She can get around a little, but she has to take it easy. She doesn't know how she's going to keep the diner going."

"Can't she hire someone to help her?" John asked. Dad looked doubtful.

"Well, she can always try," he said, "but a lot of places are looking for help these days. Sometimes it seems like there aren't enough workers to go around."

Dad knew what he was talking about. He and Mom owned a popular restaurant in New York City. It was called The Flying Rhino. Mom and Dad were always complaining about how hard it was to find people to wait on tables, cook, or wash dishes. It meant that they had to work extra hard to take up the slack. Sometimes they didn't get home till late at night.

"Things sure have changed," said Mom. "When I was growing up in Blue Harbor, Gram and Gramps had no trouble hiring high-school kids to help them out during the summer. That's when it got really busy with tourists and people from the city coming back to their summer places. In the fall, the kids would leave to go back to school, but the summer people would leave, too, and Gram and Gramps could take care of the place by themselves."

As he listened to Mom, Devin gazed at a photo of Gram's diner that was hanging on the door of the refrigerator. From the outside, Gram's diner looked something like an old railroad car. In fact, that's just what the earliest diners were—railroad dining cars that had been moved to roadside locations. Inside, there were mirrors and chrome and a lot of metal things that needed plenty of polishing to keep shiny.

"Do you think Gram would consider selling the diner?" asked Dad.

"She used to talk about it," said Mom. "But remember the time I told her that someday we'd like to move back to Maine and open a restaurant? After that, she never mentioned selling the diner. I think she's saving it for us."

"Do we want it?" asked Dad.

Mom shrugged. "Maybe," she answered.

Devin and John looked at each other with a "what's that all about?" expression on their faces.

That night Mom and Dad sat talking in the kitchen until late at night. Hearing their voices, Devin knew that something was in the air. In the morning he would find out what it was, and how much his life was about to change.

Mom and Dad explained the plan during breakfast.

Mom said, "You know how we've always talked about moving back to Maine and opening a restaurant? Well, maybe this is the time."

"Are you talking about Gram's diner?" John asked.

"Yup," said Mom. "Gram's business is OK now, especially considering that Gram only keeps it open for breakfast and lunch. Now, if I go back and make a few changes in the menu, advertise it a little more, and keep it open for longer hours, at least during the summer, maybe I can attract even more customers."

"Probably not as many as The Flying Rhino," Dad said. "But that's the whole point. We wouldn't need as many customers to make a living, because things are a lot cheaper in Maine than they are in New York City. We think that the diner could support us all with a lot less work than it takes to run our restaurant here."

"Wow," said John. "That would mean that you could spend more time with me and Devin, right?"

"Right," said Mom. "We'd be able to go to *all* your baseball games instead of just a few!"

"That is, if there's a baseball team to join in Blue Harbor," Dad said. "Don't forget, it's a small town, and there won't be as much to do there as there is to do here. We might have to drive a little to get to a museum or a movie theater."

Devin and John smiled. They liked hearing Mom and Dad talk about going to baseball games and movie theaters and museums with them. And they liked hearing about moving to Maine. Over the years the family had often talked about it, but for the first time, it was starting to seem real. And a little scary.

"Anyway," Dad went on, "Mom has decided to give it a try till fall. Gram's ankle will be healed by then. If the diner isn't working out the way we want it to, Mom will come back to New York, and Gram can keep on with the diner if she wants to."

"But what will you be doing, Dad?" Devin asked.

"I'll stay here and keep The Rhino going," Dad said, "just in case the diner doesn't work out. If it does, we'll sell The Rhino, and I'll move to Maine by winter."

"And what about me and Dev?" John asked.

Dad turned to Mom with a worried look. "I knew we were forgetting something!" he said, slapping his forehead.

Everyone laughed.

"Just kidding," Dad said. "Mom and I figure that you and Dev can make up your own minds about whether you'll go with Mom or stay here with me. School's out, so there's nothing holding you back if you want to go."

Neither Devin nor John said anything.

"Take your time," said Mom. "I won't be leaving for a couple of days yet."

That night Devin made two lists. On the list with the heading "Reasons TO Go to Maine," he wrote:

1. I like Maine.
2. I could go fishing every day.
3. I could help Mom with the diner.
4. I could do things for Gram so her broken ankle will heal.
5. I could eat fried clams every day.

On the list with the heading "Reasons NOT to Go

to Maine," Devin wrote:

1. I'd miss Dad.
2. If John doesn't go, I'd miss him, too.
3. I don't have any friends in Maine. I'd be lonely.
4. I might have to give up playing baseball for the summer.

Devin looked at his lists. He had five reasons to go to Maine and four reasons not to. Did that mean he should go? He decided to talk to John about it.

"Look at it this way," said John. "Maybe you don't have any friends in Maine. But will any of your friends be around this summer, either? I mean, Jason is on a long trip with his family, and Carlos is going to music camp for the summer, isn't he?"

John had a point. Since his two best friends would be gone, Devin might be lonely wherever he was.

"Too bad I only have two friends," Devin said sadly. But what would John know about that? It seemed to Devin that John had a trillion friends.

"Yeah, I'm sure glad I didn't get the shy gene in the family," John teased. Then he turned serious. "But that just means that you'll have to be a little more outgoing. I mean, what if there were only one other kid in the world, and he had the shy gene, too? You'd never get to be friends if one of you didn't take the first step. It might as well be you."

Devin knew that his brother was right. But he hated to be the first one to talk to someone he didn't know. That was the hardest thing of all. Once the ice was broken, though, Devin was OK, so he knew he could make friends. He just needed the other person to speak to him first.

Then Devin said, "I guess I might as well go. Even if I don't make any friends, at least I can go fishing every day. I don't need a buddy to do that. What about you? Have you decided yet?"

"I don't think I'm going," John answered. "We've got some big baseball games coming up. It's my last summer to play before I graduate from middle school, and I want to go out with a bang."

John didn't bother to remind Devin that the coach had said that John was the best shortstop he'd ever coached and that the team really needed him. So John was worried that he'd be letting the team down if he went away this summer.

"So it'll be just me and Mom, huh?" asked Devin.

"Nope," grinned John. "It'll be you, Mom, and Squeezie. You're the only one who will go near him."

Squeezie was Jason's pet python. Devin had been

able to talk Mom and Dad into letting him take care of Squeezie while Jason and his family were traveling, but not before Jason's dad reassured them that even though he was a constrictor, Squeezie wasn't at all dangerous. He was still quite small for a python.

Mom didn't see Squeezie's appeal. "What's the point of a pet you can't cuddle?" she asked. Devin joked that Squeezie did have appeal, because his skin peeled off as he grew. Mom rolled her eyes and told Devin that she'd never forgive him for such a corny joke. But for Devin's birthday, she gave him a big stuffed toy python. "It's a python you can hug without worrying about it hugging you back," she said.

After his talk with John, Devin said to Squeezie, "It's you and me, pal—off on the biggest adventure of our lives."

Squeezie was draped over a dead branch in his glass enclosure. As he gazed at Devin with eyes that looked like smooth black stones, it almost seemed to Devin that Squeezie could see into the future.

"What do you see there, fella? Is it good? Is it bad?" he asked.

But Squeezie didn't say.

3

On the Pier

So Mom, Devin, and Squeezie moved to Maine. Early on the morning of their very first day there, Mom and Devin walked down the street to the pier. Devin carried his fishing pole, tackle box, and bait bucket. He was ready for a great day of fishing.

When they got to the pier, Mom and Devin went right to Mr. Gomez' bait shack.

"Hi, Mr. Gomez," said Mom.

"Well, hello, Molly!" said Mr. Gomez, giving Mom a big hug. He had known her practically since the day she was born, and Devin could tell how glad he was to see her every year when the family came up for vacation.

"Do you remember my son, Devin?" Mom asked.

"Sure do," he said, shaking Devin's hand. "It's hard to forget a boy who likes to fish as much as he does. I'm still gobsmacked by that striper you caught last year, Devin!"

Devin blushed and smiled at Mr. Gomez' praise. Devin recalled that he had needed a lot of help from Gram to reel in that striper, but he still liked hearing Mr. Gomez' kind words.

"Now, don't forget the rules, Dev," said Mom. "When you come down to the pier, let Mr. Gomez know you're here. When you leave, say good-bye so he knows you're gone. No roughhousing on the pier. And come straight home."

"I know, Mom, I know," Devin said. He'd heard it all a million times on the drive up to Maine. He knew Mom was worried about him because this was the first year he'd be fishing by himself. On past vacations, he and Gram would come down to the pier almost every day. But it was going to be a while before Gram felt like fishing again.

Before she left to go to work at the diner, Mom nodded toward the kids fishing and whispered, "Dev, some of these kids are close to your age. Now, don't be shy. Talk to them. Who knows? Maybe you can make a friend today!"

Devin sighed. It wasn't the first time Mom had tried to nudge him into being more outgoing. It just wasn't easy for him.

Mom said good-bye, and Devin settled himself on

the pier for a morning of fishing. He threw his line in, and with no nibble to distract him, he watched the glimmer of sun on the water, the fishing boats passing by, and the clouds moving across the bright blue sky. After taking in the scenery, Devin began looking at the other kids who were fishing. They were exchanging jokes and talking with each other, but like Devin, they stood apart from each other so they wouldn't snag someone else's line.

Except for the kids fishing, the pier was quiet. Devin knew this would change as the weather got warmer and more and more summer visitors arrived in Blue Harbor. Then the pier would be crowded with people walking around in shorts and summer dresses and eating ice-cream bars from the drugstore while they waited for the ferry that would take them to one of the islands. And some of the same kids who were fishing right now might be in the water, diving for quarters and half-dollars that the tourists threw down for them.

On the Pier

Devin went back to watching the ferry. It reminded him of the boat trip to Penobscot Island that he and John took last year while Mom, Dad, and Gram got things ready for a lobster bake. They had invited lots of people, and Devin remembered feeling shy because he didn't know many of them.

It was at that moment that Devin heard the voice of the mean kid telling him, "You're in my fishing spot."

That incident happened almost a week ago, but the unfriendly kid hadn't kept Devin from going to the pier almost every day since then. If the kid was there, though, Devin tried to ignore him. So far that seemed to work pretty well, and Devin and the kid hadn't found a need to speak to each other.

4

Gram's Diner

Late one afternoon, two weeks after they arrived in Maine, Devin walked into Gram's diner on his way home from fishing. The diner had closed for the day, so except for Mom and Gram, it was empty.

"Hi, Dev," said Mom. "Did you catch any fish today?"

"Nope," Devin said. "Did you catch any customers today?"

"A few," Mom smiled. It was their little joke.

"Wash your hands and sit down, sweetie," Gram said. "Supper's almost ready."

Mom was standing at the big stove in the diner's kitchen. Her face was pink from the stove's heat, and Devin could see that her bangs were damp with sweat. She was carefully stirring something with a wooden spoon. She raised the spoon to her mouth and tasted.

Devin and Gram sat at a little table Mom had set up in the kitchen. Gram was knitting watch caps.

A lot of women in town did. They sold them in the local craft shops and even in the drugstore. Fishermen and people who spent any time outdoors bought them to keep their heads warm and dry, and visitors to Maine often bought them as souvenirs.

"Oh, Devin," Mom said brightly, "I was bringing some of Gram's watch caps to the store today, and I met someone else who was bringing in caps. Her name is Denise Costa."

"Do you mean Denise Toothaker?" Gram asked. "Ada Toothaker's daughter?"

"That's right, Gram," said Mom. "At least, that was her name until she married Joe Costa. He was from Massachusetts. Remember?"

"That's right," said Gram. "He was a fisherman in Gloucester. That's where they moved after they got married."

"Well, she's back now," said Mom. "Her husband died when his boat sank during a storm. So sad. Anyway, a couple of months ago she and her son Danny moved into an apartment. She doesn't know quite what she wants to do to make a living yet— maybe she'll go back to school to learn computer skills or something. She was a waitress in Gloucester, but for now she's happy just making watch caps. It doesn't pay much money—"

"Don't I know it!" Gram said under her breath.

"—but at least it lets her spend a lot of time with Danny. Danny's about your age, Dev," Mom went on. "Denise said that he hasn't made any friends yet. He's kind of shy."

Devin waited for Mom to add, "like you, Dev." He was glad when she didn't. He got tired of being reminded that he was shy.

Mom kept on stirring as she talked. Devin and Gram watched curiously as she tasted the mixture again, sprinkled in some cinnamon, stirred, and tasted yet again.

"Mmmm," she said. "I think you'll like this. It's a sauce for salmon. Dad says it's a big hit at The Rhino. Maybe I'll add it to the menu at the diner."

Devin and Gram looked at each other. Mom thought that if they added a few "interesting" dishes to the diner's menu, they might "catch" more customers. Gram and Devin were usually the taste-testers.

"We ought to get T-shirts that say *guinea pigs,*" Gram whispered to Devin. "Molly," Gram went on, "if you want to add salmon to the menu, great. But people here will like it better if you keep it simple. Just broil it or steam it and serve it with a slice of lemon."

"Gram, you're behind the times," Mom answered.

"People who go to restaurants today like their food to taste interesting and different. They like sauces and different herbs and spices. Especially people from the city, and there are lots of city folks here in the summer."

Gram had an answer to Mom's argument. "Just maybe," she said, "city folks like city things when they're living in the city and small-town things when they're vacationing in a small town. Well," she went on, "I've told you before, you can make any changes you want, if you think it'll improve business."

If some of Gram's customers had heard her, they would have protested. Gram once told Devin that when she mentioned to one of her "regulars" that she might do a little remodeling to spiff up the place, he joked that if she changed anything, he'd never come back.

Some people took their diners seriously, Devin knew, especially an old-fashioned one like Gram's. In fact, a couple of years earlier a fellow stopped at Gram's and told her that he was traveling all over the country taking pictures of old-time diners for a book he was writing. Gram let him take all the pictures he wanted and then signed a form giving him permission to publish them in his book. The man promised to send Gram a copy of the book when it came out, but that had been so long ago that Gram said she had quit hoping for it.

Mom was still stirring. "Gram," she said, "I wouldn't change anything about the diner except the menu. Now you two get ready for some delicious salmon."

Mom took the salmon out of the steamer. It was a beautiful pinky-orange color. After putting some on Gram and Devin's plates, she dribbled some of the pale sauce on it. The sauce had bits of green in it. Basil? wondered Devin.

"Tell me what you think," she said.

Devin and Gram cut off pieces of salmon with their forks. They raised them to their mouths and chewed thoughtfully.

Devin looked at Gram and then at Mom. Then he said, "You want my honest opinion, Mom? Cinnamon makes salmon taste like it wants to be cookies. I think salmon's better with plain old lemon juice."

Gram hid a smile behind her hand. Mom made a face at her and said, "What does he know? His favorite food is macaroni and cheese from a box."

Gram laughed. "Mine too!" she said.

After supper Devin and Gram helped Mom get ready for what Mom called "the breakfast crowd."

Mom once said to Gram that it was probably a good thing that they didn't get all that many customers, because she couldn't afford to hire anyone to work at the diner, even if she *could* find someone. So Mom had to do everything herself, from waiting on tables to cooking to clearing tables and washing dishes. That's why Devin tried to help as much as he could.

While Mom got the big coffeemaker ready, Devin set the tables and replenished the rack that held little boxes of cereal. Gram sat at a booth with her broken

ankle propped up as she refilled the sugar containers
and poured water from a pitcher into little vases. In
the morning Mom would fill them with flowers she
had just picked from Gram's garden and put them on
the tables.

Devin was about to lift a rack of coffee mugs and
carry it into the dining area when Mom stopped him.

"I'll carry that, honey," she said. "It looks a little
heavy for you. Would you get some bacon from the
freezer for me?"

"OK, Mom," said Devin. He knew that Mom remembered that he had dropped a tray of glasses the week before. What a mess! It had taken Mom at least a half hour to pick up all the little shards of glass. She wouldn't let Devin help because she was afraid he would cut himself.

Devin went into the big walk-in freezer to get the bacon. He put several packages in the refrigerator to thaw. Then he helped Mom mop the blue-and-white tiled floor of the diner.

At last the diner was all cleaned and polished and ready for the next day. All Mom would have to do is unlock the door at six o'clock, make coffee, fix the flower vases, and wait for the "breakfast crowd."

Just as Mom was locking the door, Devin said, "Just a second, Mom—I think I forgot to turn the freezer light off."

He went back inside. When he came back out he said, "It's a good thing I checked—the light was on!"

"Good thing is right," Mom said. "You probably saved me a quarter in electricity!"

"Just put it in my piggy bank," Devin answered.

5

The Mishap

The next day, Devin got up before his mother and grandmother. After eating a bowl of cereal, he fixed himself a peanut butter sandwich and put it in his backpack. Then he grabbed his fishing pole and tackle box, put on his baseball cap, and set out for the pier. Peering through the early morning fog, Devin could see that quite a few people were already there. That told him that the tide was high—the best time for fishing.

After buying some raw clams from Mr. Gomez, Devin sat in his usual spot—the one he found for himself after getting scolded by the dark-haired boy. He carefully tied a sinker onto his line. Then he attached a bobber and baited his hook with a clam. The sinker made a soft plunk as he dropped his line into the water. Devin waited to see if the bait would attract any nibbles. That gave him a chance to look around at his fellow fishermen.

There were about twelve of them. They were

talking and laughing, but Devin wasn't able to hear much of what they were saying. He wondered if they were talking about him.

Devin wished he could say something to the boy who was closest to him. He knew it wouldn't take much—just "Catch anything yet?" or "What's that lure you're using?" Almost anything he might say could lead to a conversation and—just maybe—a new friend. But Devin couldn't open his mouth.

Then Devin noticed someone else—the dark-haired boy. He was sitting quietly, leaning against the piling that had first attracted Devin to that spot. That explained why Devin hadn't seen him at first—his dark shirt blended in with the piling, and he almost looked like part of the pier.

No wonder no one's talking to him, Devin thought. He's so mean that no one probably wants anything to do with him. Then Devin remembered that no one was talking to him, either. Did that mean that no one wanted anything to do with *him?*

After a couple of hours, Devin hadn't caught anything. Deciding that he was hungry even if the fish weren't, he ate his peanut butter sandwich for a snack. Then he fished for two more hours before giving up.

As he waved good-bye to Mr. Gomez, the man called out, "Too bad, Dev! Better luck tomorrow!"

The Mishap

The other kids looked up from their spots and Devin blushed. Did Mr. Gomez have to advertise that Devin hadn't caught anything? Why wasn't he shouting like that when he talked about the striper that Devin had caught last year?

But by the time Devin got to the corner of his street, he had forgotten about Mr. Gomez and instead was looking forward to the grilled cheese and tomato sandwich that Mom had promised to fix him for lunch.

As soon as Devin got to the door of the diner he saw a big sign that said CLOSED FOR THE DAY. His stomach fell. Something about the letters looked angry. Maybe it was their color—bright red.

Devin walked into the diner. Gram was sitting at a table with a cup of coffee in front of her. The look she gave Devin was half a smile and half a frown.

"Your mom's in the kitchen," she said.

Mom was doing something at the sink.

"Hey, Mom. What's up?" Devin asked. He spoke as casually as he could, but his stomach was churning. Mom raised her head. The look she gave him was a lot like Gram's.

Devin looked around for a clue to what the problem was. He soon found one—a big box of steaks sitting on top of the garbage pail. The pail was overflowing with dripping packages of formerly frozen vegetables, meats, and ice cream.

Devin realized right away what had happened.

"Oh no!" he said. "I turned off the freezer instead of the freezer light!"

Mom didn't say anything. She knew she didn't need to scold Devin. He would do a great job of scolding himself.

When Mom got back from the diner that night, she found Devin sitting glumly on the front steps.

"Hey, sport," she said, sitting beside him. "I've got good news. The damage wasn't as bad as we thought. Not everything was spoiled. We have enough food to open the diner tomorrow. I can call in an order for what we need for the rest of the week."

"Boy, Mom, I really messed up," Devin said. "Instead of saving you twenty-five cents on electricity, I cost you a whole lot of money on spoiled food. And in lost customers because you had to keep the diner closed."

"So?" answered Mom. "Everyone messes up sometimes. Forget about it. You're a big help to me. I'm really glad you're here.

"I'm bushed. I think I'm heading straight to bed. Good night, honey." Mom hugged Devin's shoulders and kissed him on the cheek.

"Good night, Mom," said Devin.

Unless it was Sunday and the diner was closed, Mom always spent some time looking at the account book before she went to bed. The account book was where she kept track of how much money the diner took in each day. Tonight she was going straight to bed because there was nothing to write in the book for that day. The diner had been closed—because of Devin.

Devin didn't usually take his stuffed python to bed with him. But tonight he did.

6

Devin Helps Gram

When Gram came downstairs the next morning, Devin had just fixed himself a bowl of cereal.

"Well," Gram said, ruffling his hair, "I'm surprised to see you here this time of day. You're usually off fishing by now."

"Mr. Gomez is out lobstering with his son today," Devin answered. "I'm not allowed to fish from the pier unless he's there."

"So you'll have to spend a dull day at home," Gram teased, "with nobody but me and Squeezie for company."

Gram poured herself a cup of coffee. "How are things going?" she asked Devin.

Devin stared at his cereal bowl. After what had happened the day before, he felt pretty discouraged. He wanted to say, "Things are awful. I try to help Mom, but all I do is mess up. I break glasses and I turn off the freezer. If the restaurant doesn't work out, it'll probably be all my fault. Besides, I miss Dad and John. I don't have any friends here. I'll probably never have any friends here. I'm lonely. Sometimes I wish I hadn't come." That's what Devin *wanted* to say. But instead he just said, "OK."

Gram didn't reply. Devin looked up at her. She was looking straight into his eyes. Her clear blue eyes were like Mom's—they seemed like they could see right through him.

Devin felt as if Gram had understood everything he had wanted to say, even though he hadn't said it.

Later that day Gram said, "Devin, would you mind helping me this afternoon? I've got some yarn I need to roll up. You can hold it for me."

"Sure thing, Gram," Devin said. He was glad to help her, but he couldn't help thinking that she was just giving him busywork—something to make him feel useful and at the same time keep him from causing any more trouble.

Devin sat on the top step of the front porch with the navy-blue yarn draped over his hands. Gram sat above him in a rocking chair, rolling the yarn into a ball. From time to time Devin looked at the gulls soaring overhead, squawking as they chased each other over bits of food.

"Your mom served her salmon sauce at lunch today," said Gram. "I wonder how it went over."

Devin smiled. He'd have to remember to ask Mom about the sauce at supper tonight.

"I just hope she doesn't give up on macaroni and cheese," he said.

"Or meatloaf with mashed potatoes," grinned Gram.

"One thing I wish she'd give up on are those home-fried potatoes with—what is that green stuff she puts on them?" asked Devin.

"Rosemary," said Gram. "It's an herb—a plant."

"Whatever," commented Devin. "It makes them taste like soap. Lots of people in New York seem to like them, though. You should see them lined up outside The Rhino for brunch on Saturday and Sunday mornings."

Somebody was walking by the house. Devin turned his head to see who it was.

Oh no. It was that mean dark-haired boy. He had his fishing rod over his shoulder, and in his bait bucket, Devin could see the tails of several fish.

The boy looked at Devin, and Devin thought he

saw a sneer on his face. Devin didn't blame him for sneering. There he was, returning in triumph from the pier, fat fish in his bucket. And there was Devin, Mr. No-Can-Catch-'Em, fiddling with yarn and talking about recipes. Devin was so embarrassed that he wanted to disappear into thin air.

Gram saw the boy, too.

"Good afternoon!" she sang out. When Gram was sitting on her porch, she was the street's unofficial greeter.

"Hi," the boy answered. Then he put his head down and seemed to slink past the house.

"I wonder who that boy is," Gram said.

Devin was surprised. "I thought you said you knew everyone in Blue Harbor, Gram," he said.

"Well, I was wrong," Gram said. "I know *almost* everyone in Blue Harbor. I never saw *him* before."

"Gram," said Devin, "remember that kid I told you about? The kid who kicked me out of his fishing spot? That was him."

"Oh, really?" asked Gram. "Well, for sure that spot didn't belong to his father or grandfather because they didn't come from Blue Harbor. I'd know him if they had. Nope, he's laid claim to that spot all by himself."

From the way Gram spoke, she seemed to admire the boy because of the way he went after what he wanted.

"Say," said Gram, "you don't think that's Denise Costa's boy, do you? The one your mom was telling us about? Danny, I think his name is."

"Huh," said Devin, sounding uninterested. But his mind was racing. If that was Danny, then he was new in town. And shy, according to his mother. So maybe that was why he was alone all the time and didn't talk to anyone at the pier.

Just like Devin.

7

Lost-and-Found

That night, before he went to sleep, Devin remembered what John had said. Two shy kids would never become friends unless one of them took the first step. He was still thinking about it on the way to the pier the next morning.

Devin was trying to see the dark-haired boy in a whole different light. If the boy was really Danny Costa, maybe he wasn't really mean. Maybe he was just making a place for himself as a new boy in a new town. On the other hand, maybe he *wasn't* Danny Costa, and maybe he *was* really mean. Devin needed to find out which it was. A lot depended on it. He just hoped he was brave enough. If the boy was mean, he might get REALLY mean if Devin said the wrong thing to him—especially after he had seen Devin knitting on the front porch with Gram yesterday. Well, not really knitting, but the next thing to it.

There you go, thinking yourself into a box again, Devin said to himself. Just say something to the kid.

Devin had been looking at the ground while he walked, but now he lifted his head. There was the dark-haired boy, walking half a block ahead of him. Devin walked a little further and saw something on the ground. It was a knife, the kind people use to cut bait with.

Devin picked it up. Did the boy drop it? he wondered. Asking him would be a good reason to talk to him. Devin's heart swelled with courage.

But by the time Devin got to the pier, his courage had seeped out of him. So instead of taking the knife over to the boy, Devin took it to Mr. Gomez, who kept a box filled with sunglasses, sweaters, jackets, caps, and other items people had left on the pier.

"Thanks, Devin," Mr. Gomez said. "Looks like a nice knife. Hope the owner claims it. If not, it's yours in a month."

Devin went to his fishing spot feeling very disappointed in himself. He hadn't even had the courage to ask the kid if he had dropped a knife, for Pete's sake.

As he began to fish, Devin watched the boy out of the corner of his eye. After a few minutes, he saw the kid begin to rummage in his tackle box. Then the boy stood up and fished in his pockets. Finally he looked all around him and even began to retrace his steps along the pier.

Devin wished that Mr. Gomez wasn't distracted by a customer. If Mr. Gomez would only look over and see the kid, he would probably call out, "Looking for something?" For the kid's part, it didn't seem to occur to him to ask Mr. Gomez about the knife. He probably doesn't even know that Mr. Gomez keeps a lost-and-found box, Devin told himself.

Devin even tried sending the kid thought waves about Mr. Gomez. It didn't work, and the kid kept searching along the pier.

Finally Devin couldn't stand it anymore. He stood up and walked over to the kid.

"Did you lose something?" Devin asked him.

"A knife," said the boy.

"Check with Mr. Gomez," muttered Devin. Then he turned away without saying another word.

Devin fished for a while without catching anything. Finally he packed up his fishing gear and started home. At that exact moment, the dark-haired kid started for home, too. The kid looked up at Devin and said, "Hi. Are you headed home?"

"Yup," said Devin. Boy, was he surprised.

"We live on the same street," the kid went on to say as he packed up his gear. "I saw you on your porch yesterday."

Devin waited for a nasty joke about knitting. None came.

Now Devin and the boy were walking together on their way home.

"Mr. Gomez told me that you turned in my knife," he said. "Thanks!"

Devin nodded. He didn't want to take too much credit. He was still angry at himself for not just bringing the knife to the kid in the first place.

The boys introduced themselves. Gram was right—the kid's name was Danny Costa.

"Did you catch anything today?" Danny asked.

"No," said Devin. "How about you?"

"Nah," he answered.

Devin's shyness had disappeared, and the boys chatted all the way home. Danny seemed nice enough to Devin. He wondered why Danny had been so mean on the pier that first day. He decided to wait before asking that question.

When they got to Devin's house, Devin said, "I'm

taking care of a friend's pet python. Do you want to see him?"

Danny looked surprised. For a second he didn't seem sure whether he wanted to see the snake or not. Then he said, "OK."

Devin led Danny to the kitchen. As usual, Gram was sitting at the table with her foot propped up, knitting a watch cap. That's how she spent a lot of her time, now that she had to keep off her ankle.

Devin introduced Danny to Gram. Then he said, "I'm going to introduce Danny to Squeezie, too. Oh, and is it OK if I soak Squeezie in the bathtub?"

"OK," said Gram. "But remember not to take your eyes off him! The last thing I want is a python on the loose."

"Trust me," grinned Devin.

Gram said, "I usually never trust anyone who says 'trust me.' But for you, I'll make an exception."

Devin kept Squeezie in his bedroom, in a big glass case that had a secure lid. Mom had made sure of that before she had said yes to Devin's request to watch the snake for the summer.

As he and Danny peered in at the snake, Devin said, "He's really neat and no trouble at all. All I need to do is clean his enclosure, make sure he always has a big bowl of fresh water, feed him once in a while, and let him get a good soaking sometimes."

Devin took the top off the enclosure and lifted Squeezie out. The python draped himself over Devin's shoulders like a thick scarf.

"Cool," Danny said as he touched Squeezie's smooth skin.

"See?" said Devin. "He outgrows his old skin. That's why I have to soak him. It helps him get his old skin off."

Devin carried Squeezie into the bathroom. The bathtub was full of plants.

"Yikes!" he said. "Mom's watering Gram's ferns. Oh, well. No problem. We have a big sink at the diner. I can soak him there."

"Are you sure your mom won't mind?" Danny asked.

"Nah. It's Sunday, so the diner's closed. Anyway, she's there now. I can ask her."

Devin put Squeezie into a cloth laundry bag. Then he slung the bag over his shoulder for the short walk to the diner.

The back door to the diner was open, but Mom wasn't there.

"She must have gone out for a second," said

Devin. "She'll be back soon, or she would've locked the door. Come on in, the sink's right here."

Devin and Danny cleared some pots and pans out of the stainless steel sink. Then Devin filled it half full with warm water and put Squeezie in. Just his head was hanging over the edge of the sink.

"See how his tongue is flicking in and out?" asked Devin. "That means he's smelling something."

"Maybe your mom's cooking," said Danny.

"Or maybe he smells a mouse," joked Devin.

A loud crash sent Devin and Danny running to the back door of the diner. It was Mom. She had dropped a stack of baking pans she had been carrying from the car. Devin quickly introduced Danny while they helped her pick up the pans and pile them on a counter in the kitchen.

"So you're Denise's son," Mom said. "I've met your mom, and I'm very glad to meet *you!*" She gave Devin a pleased look. "Good going!" it seemed to say.

"Hey, Mom," Devin said as he nested several loaf pans inside each other, "wait'll you see who we've got in the sink!"

"*Who* you've got in the sink?" Mom asked. Oh-oh, thought Devin. Mom's invisible antennas were bristling from her head. She sensed trouble.

"Yeah," he hurried to reassure her. "It's Squeezie. The bathtub was full of ferns, and . . ."

"Squeezie?" shrieked Mom. Like a shot, she was at the door of the kitchen. Mom looked anxiously across the room at Squeezie's bathing spot, the sink.

Squeezie wasn't there.

8

A Python Is Missing

Devin didn't sleep much that night. He had gone to bed early after he, Mom, and Danny thoroughly searched the diner. They didn't find Squeezie. Devin knew that Squeezie could survive for a long, long time by catching the mice that Mom sometimes had to set traps for. Devin remembered that once Squeezie disappeared for two weeks in Jason's house. Eventually the family discovered him in a closet. In the meantime, the diner would have to stay closed, its doors and windows securely locked.

Devin's mind was racing. "I've ruined us," he said to himself. "I've ruined the family. There's no way we'll ever get this diner going. Especially now. We'll probably have to keep the diner closed for weeks. We haven't got a chance. Mom and Dad will never forgive me. Neither will Gram. They'll probably send me to

Siberia. No, further. They'll probably send me to the moon. Even NASA won't be able to find me."

The next morning Devin got up early and went to the diner, hoping to catch Squeezie. No luck. Devin went to the pier, where Danny was already fishing.

"Hi, Danny," Devin said as he walked past.

"Hi," said Danny. "Still no Squeezie?"

"Nope," said Devin.

Later, Danny stopped by Devin's fishing spot.

"Hey, Devin," he said, "I'm leaving. I promised Mom I'd be home for lunch. She said I could invite you, if you want to come."

The invitation brightened Devin's mood.

"Sure," he said.

During the short walk home Danny said, "Let's hurry. I don't want to be late. Mom said she was going to 'sweep the kitchen' today. That's my favorite lunch."

"Huh?" Devin said. " 'Sweep the kitchen'? What's that mean?"

Danny laughed. "That's diner talk," he said. "I forget that not everyone speaks it. It means she's going to make hash."

"You mean diners have their own language?"

Danny shrugged. "Not so much anymore, I guess. But years and years ago people who used to work in diners had crazy names for different foods. Mom used to work in a diner in Gloucester. They still used diner lingo there, and she got a kick out of it. She still uses it."

When they reached Devin's house, Devin went inside to tell the grown-ups where he was going. Mom was in the kitchen talking on the phone. Devin couldn't hear exactly what she was saying, but he caught the word "snake." He guessed that she was talking to Dad, and he was relieved that he didn't have to stay around.

"Gram, Danny's mom invited me for lunch. Can I go?" he asked.

Gram nodded. "I think that would be a very good idea," she answered solemnly.

"Danny says his mom's going to 'sweep the kitchen' today," Devin went on.

Gram threw her head back and laughed. "You mean she's going to make hash? I haven't heard that expression for ages."

Devin helped Gram fix supper that night. Macaroni and cheese—both their favorites. Mom was hanging around the diner, hoping Squeezie would make a move and betray his whereabouts. After supper, it would be Devin's turn to look around.

"How was the hash you had for lunch?" Gram asked.

"Great!" Devin said. "You know what we had for dessert?"

"No. What?" Gram asked.

" 'Fish eyes,' " said Devin.

"Tapioca!" said Gram, laughing.

After a minute Gram said, "It's certainly nice that you've found a friend."

"Yup!" answered Devin. "I can't believe I thought he was such a mean kid at first. But I keep forgetting to ask him why he kicked me out of his fishing spot the first day I saw him."

Gram smiled. "Someday you'll find out," she said.

9

Gotcha!

Three nights later, Devin was lying in bed, thinking. Squeezie still hadn't turned up. It looked like the diner would have to stay closed again tomorrow—the fifth full day.

Now Devin was really getting worried. That afternoon he had overheard Mom and Gram talking about the diner. Gram had said that by now even their regular customers would have found other places to get their coffee and pie and sandwiches and iced tea. So that meant that besides getting new customers, they would have to win back the old ones. This is a huge mess! thought Devin.

A loud clank distracted Devin from his worries. Then he heard another sound—a crash. The noises seemed to come from the diner.

Squeezie? Devin wondered. Hunting a mouse? He got out of bed and crept downstairs. The house was dark and quiet. His mother and grandmother were both asleep.

Devin took the key to the diner from the nail beside the kitchen door. Then he walked the short distance across the lawn to the diner's back door.

A short time later, police officers Bob Downlander and Sharon Bouchard burst through that same door. They were met with a strange sight, they later told Devin's mom.

Devin, in his pajamas, was standing in the middle of the kitchen floor. Pots and pans were everywhere,

some of them dented. Triumphant and grinning, he had a thick python slung across his shoulders.

"Tah-daaah!" he sang out.

"It's kind of strange," Devin said to Danny on their way to the pier the next morning. "Last night when I went to bed at 9:00, I felt like the family villain. Then the snake thing happened, and when I came down for breakfast this morning, I was a hero. Mom gave me a big hug. Gram made me pancakes. They didn't even care about the dented pots and pans!"

Danny shook his head in puzzlement. "There's just no telling," he said. "What about Squeezie?"

"He's banned from the diner," said Devin. "He's not allowed in there ever again."

Danny nodded as if that made good sense to him.

As the boys got closer to the pier, Devin noticed a big banner strung across Main Street. Something was written on it in huge letters.

" 'Lobster Festival,' " Devin read aloud. " 'July 14th.' What's that?"

"It's a festival they have in the park every July."

The boys were startled to hear Mr. Gomez' voice. He had been walking behind them without their realizing it. "Hordes of people come from all over the place. They have booths selling lobster—steamed lobster, baked lobster, fried lobster, lobster chowder, lobster casserole, lobster salad—lobster any way you can imagine and a few you can't. Other kinds of food, too—hot dogs, hamburgers, fish sandwiches, clams, onion rings, french fries—you name it. And crafts. It's a lot of fun. Hope to see you there!" he said as he went to open his bait shack.

"Hmmm," said Devin. "We've always come up to Blue Harbor in August. I wonder if Mom knows about the Lobster Festival. Maybe she could have a food booth with something from the diner. It might be good advertising. And if it's something really delicious, people will come to the diner to have more of it."

"What kind of food?" Danny asked. "Something like salmon with cinnamon sauce?" Devin had told

Danny and his mother about some of Mom's recipes when he had been at their house for lunch.

"Pull-*eeez!*" Devin said. "Nope, we need *real* food—food that little kids would pester their moms and dads for as soon as they saw our booth. Something that wouldn't cost very much. Like a dessert."

"Yum!" said Danny. "I'll taste-test dessert anytime!"

10

Cake and Ice Cream

"...**A**nd Gram and Danny and I could take care of the booth. You wouldn't even have to close the diner that day, Mom." Devin was trying to talk Mom into having a booth at the festival.

"What do you think, Gram?" Mom asked. She had been poring over the account book with a worried frown on her face, but she put it aside for a few minutes to listen to Devin.

"I've never had a booth at the festival," Gram said. "It always seemed like a lot of work for one person. But I think it's a good idea. Especially if we can come up with something really good to sell. Like Devin said, something that would make people come to the diner for more."

"Let's do it," Mom said. "It might be fun, and it might even make a little money. From the look of things," she said, gesturing to the account book, "we need it. I'm afraid we're not doing very well."

Devin knew how discouraged Mom was about how the diner was going. Even before the Great Snake Escape, it had begun to lose ground. Now it was making even less than Gram had made when she was running it by herself. Mom couldn't imagine what the problem was. She had eliminated some of the dishes Gram had been serving for years and replaced them with some of the most popular dishes at The Rhino, but still people stayed away in droves.

"Well," Mom went on, "what should we sell? Clam chowder?"

"I think we should sell a dessert," said Devin. "Kids like dessert, and not every kid likes clam chowder."

"That's true," said Mom. "We should have something the whole family would like—a good, old-fashioned dessert. Bread pudding?"

"Too plain," said Gram.

"Brownies?" suggested Devin.

"Too ordinary," said Mom. "Cookies?"

"Talk about ordinary," said Gram. "How about a nice old-fashioned chocolate cake?"

"Perfect!" said Mom. "A moist, buttery, delicious

cake, made from scratch, just the way you used to make when I was a kid, Gram."

"With thick, gooey chocolate frosting!" added Devin. He was glad to see his mom's enthusiasm for his idea about the booth. The summer was running down, and he was afraid that before too many more weeks, she would be sitting him down for a talk about how the diner wasn't working out, and they'd better go back to New York and stick with The Rhino. Not that going back would be awful. After all, Dad and John were there. But still, the thought of leaving Danny and Gram and the people he was getting to know in Blue Harbor made Devin sad. It was beginning to feel like home.

"I've still got that old recipe of my grandmother's that I used to make," said Gram. "But it might take me awhile to find it. I haven't made it in years. If people like the cake, we could add it to the menu at the diner.

"You know what would be fun?" Gram went on. "Since we're going to be selling an old-fashioned chocolate cake, we should dress in old-fashioned clothes. It might make the cake taste even better. And it would sure get people's attention—sort of like advertising. I've got plenty of old clothes in the attic."

"Great idea, Gram," Mom said as she and Devin

high-fived. "There's no stopping us now!"

Devin and Danny laughed as they pawed through an old trunk in Gram's attic. They were looking for clothes to wear while they ran the booth at the Lobster Festival.

"How about these?" Devin asked, holding up what looked like very short pants.

"They're weird," said Danny. "They're too short to be pants and too long to be shorts."

"That's because they're knickers!" said Devin. "I saw a picture of my great-grandpa wearing some, and they came to just below his knees. Look, here's another pair for you!"

"Oh, great!" said Danny sarcastically. "I wouldn't be caught dead in those!"

"Come on, it's just for a day!" said Devin, surprising himself. Someone—usually Mom—often had to tell *him* not to take things so seriously.

"Great-grandpa was wearing a pair of kneesocks with them," Devin went on. "I wonder . . ." He paused to rummage in a corner of the trunk. "Yup! I found some!"

Danny was looking in a little closet. He came out

carrying something on a hanger that was wrapped in plastic. "Hey, here's a black dress," he said. "Is it the one your grandmother asked us to look for?"

"Let's check the photo," said Devin. Gram had given them a photograph of her mother wearing the dress she hoped they would find.

"Yup! There's the same white collar. That's the one!"

"What's that bucket thing she's cranking in the picture?" Danny asked.

"Gram said it's what they used in the olden days to make ice cream. You put cream and ice and other stuff in it and crank it for a long time, and *voila!*—delicious ice cream. She said that when her ankle's better she'll come up and look for it so we can make ice cream."

"Wow," said Danny.

"That gives me an idea," said Devin. "What goes perfectly with old-fashioned, gooey chocolate cake?"

"Vanilla ice cream?" asked Danny.

"Right!" said Devin. "Old-fashioned vanilla ice cream made from scratch with an old-fashioned ice-cream maker. What could be better? Let's see if we can find that thing."

Devin and Danny searched and searched. Finally they found the ice-cream maker on the top shelf in the closet where Danny had found Gram's dress. It was dusty and the handle needed to be oiled, but otherwise it was in perfect shape.

"We'd better find out how to make ice cream before we say anything to Mom about it," Devin said.

Devin and Danny took the ice-cream maker downstairs. Danny began to clean it up while Devin got out Gram's oldest cookbook.

"1927!" he read on the copyright page. "This thing is an antique! Let's see," he said, looking in the index. "Ice Cream—pages 566 to 575." Turning the pages eagerly, Devin found the recipe he was looking for.

"'Vanilla Ice Cream,'" he read. "Hey, listen to this, Danny! This is easy! We only need cream, vanilla, sugar, and a little salt. This recipe is a piece of cake!"

"No," corrected Danny, "it's *for* a piece of cake."

"Look, it's got other flavors, too," said Devin. "Apricot, grape, orange, banana, burnt walnut . . . It says you put all the ingredients here," Devin went on, pointing to the metal can that Danny was holding. "Then you put the can in the wooden tub and pack ice and salt around it. When you turn the handle, the can turns, and the stuff in the can freezes into ice cream! Mom's gonna *love* this idea!" Devin went on.

"Yeah," said Danny. "She'll probably even want to help!"

Danny's words made Devin look up from Gram's cookbook. "Whoa," he said. "You're right. Mom probably *would* want to help. In fact, she'd probably insist on helping—especially after the mess I've made of things lately. And she's got enough to do already." After a couple of seconds Devin said, "On second thought, let's have the ice-cream caper be our little secret."

11

Top Secret

"**N**inety-six, ninety-seven, ninety-eight, ninety-nine, one hundred!" Devin counted the last of the coins excitedly. "That makes $78 and—let's see—18 cents! That should be plenty to buy what we need!"

Devin and Danny sat on the floor of Devin's bedroom, surrounded by bills and coins. Devin's piggybank lay overturned and empty on the floor between them. Even so, the grin on the pig's face made it look proud and satisfied.

"Now all we need to do is make a shopping list and make a plan," Devin said.

Just then the boys heard a door close.

"Shhhh!" Danny whispered. "That might be your mom! Where can we go?"

"To my house!" said Danny.

"Let's go!" said Devin.

"Hand-cranked ice cream? That's a lot of work!" Mrs. Costa said. "You guys are going to need extra muscle power. Want some help?"

"That would be great! Thanks, Mrs. Costa!" Devin said.

"You're welcome," grinned Mrs. Costa. "I'm getting tired of knitting, anyway. Still, gotta make a living, however humble. When do we start?"

Mrs. Costa yanked a length of yarn from the ball that was hidden in the knitting bag beside her.

"Here, Danny," she said, holding out a hank of yarn. "I'm almost out of yarn. Hold this for me while I roll some up, will you?"

Devin smiled to himself as Danny draped the yarn over his hands and Mrs. Costa began to roll it up. So that's why he never teased me about it, he thought. Probably all the kids in town have to hold yarn for their moms and grandmothers.

"So when do we start?" Mrs. Costa asked again.

"Well, first we have to figure out how much stuff we have to buy . . ." Devin began.

"After you do that, let me know," said Mrs. Costa. "I can drive you to the grocery store. And let's see . . ." Mrs. Costa had abruptly put down her ball of yarn, walked over to a cupboard under the sink and began rummaging through it.

"Here!" she said triumphantly as she pulled out a tall stack of plastic ice-cream containers. "I knew I was saving these for something!

"Now," she said, "all this talk of delicious, hand-cranked ice cream has made me hungry. Besides, it's getting close to suppertime. Devin, why don't you call your mom and ask if you can stay. Danny and I will walk you home later."

"Thanks, Mrs. Costa," said Devin.

"Don't thank me until after you've had supper," said Mrs. Costa. "Now, what shall we eat tonight?"

"How about 'burning a few,' Mom?" said Danny.

"I think I can do that," said Mrs. Costa. "Shall I 'drag them through the garden and pin a rose on them'?" she asked.

"Sure!" said Danny.

By now both Danny and Mrs. Costa were laughing at Devin's look of puzzlement.

"That means that Mom's going to fix hamburgers with lettuce, tomato, and onion," explained Danny.

"And for dessert, maybe I'll whip up some 'nervous pudding,'" said Mrs. Costa. She and Danny looked at Devin and waited for him to figure it out.

"Does it start with a *J?*" Devin asked.

"Bingo!" said Mrs. Costa.

With Mrs. Costa's help, by the next afternoon Devin and Danny had gathered the ingredients for their first batch of ice cream. There they were—the cream, the vanilla flavoring, the sugar, the rock salt, and the table salt, neatly arranged on Danny's kitchen table. The other stuff they needed was there, too—a bag of ice, a scoop for measuring the ice and the rock salt, a wooden mallet and canvas bag for crushing the ice, and the ice-cream maker.

"Let's see," said Devin as he read Gram's cookbook. "First we need to mix a quart of cream, one-and-a-half tablespoons of vanilla, three-quarters of a cup of sugar, and a little salt."

"Easy," said Danny.

In no time the mixture was ready to freeze in the ice-cream maker.

"Now comes the tricky part," said Devin. "It says to crush the ice with the mallet in a canvas bag until the pieces are about the size of the rock salt."

"I'll get started on that," Danny said, and soon the kitchen was ringing with the crunching sound of a mallet hitting a bag of ice.

"That's good enough," said Devin. "Now we fill

the can of the ice-cream maker two-thirds full with the stuff we just mixed."

"Done," said Danny.

"Great. Next we fill the tub one-third full with the ice. Yikes!" Devin said as some of the ice in the scoop Danny was wielding clattered to the floor.

"Now we put alternate layers of rock salt and ice up to the top of the can," he went on.

"Does it matter whether the salt or the ice is on top?" Danny asked.

"I don't think so," said Devin. "We just have to make sure it's packed in tight. I'll bang it down a little with the mallet. There!"

"Now we can start cranking, right?" asked Danny.

"Let's see—nope! We have to let it sit for five minutes," answered Devin.

"Good!" said Danny. "Just enough time to make a peanut butter sandwich. I'm starved! Do you want one?"

"Sure!" said Devin.

Five minutes later, Devin was looking in the cookbook again.

"It says to turn the crank slowly and steadily for five or ten minutes until the stuff is frozen into a mush, and then faster until it's hard to turn. That'll mean that the stuff is frozen. Want me to turn first?"

"Go ahead," said Danny. "I'll take the second shift."

When all the cranking had been done, the boys took the lid off the metal can that held the ice cream. They each took a spoonful for their first taste.

"Hmmmm," said Devin. "What do you think?"

"Hmmmm," said Danny. "Very tasty. But I think we need to practice some more."

12

Cake Batter

Devin walked into the kitchen of his house. "Hi, Gram!" he said.

"I was just beginning to wonder where you were," said Gram.

"We were making ice cream at Danny's," said Devin. He had already told Gram about the secret project so she wouldn't worry about him being away from home so much.

"My gosh," Gram said. "That's four days in a row! And the festival is only two days away! Don't you have enough yet?"

"Not really," said Devin. "We only have about ten quarts. It took a while to learn to make it right. Our first few batches came out a little funny. They tasted great, but they were kind of crunchy. It turned out we were turning the crank too fast, and little chunks of ice formed in the ice cream. But we've got it figured out now," he said. "Anyway, we had fun eating the practice ice cream. What's for supper tonight?"

"'Bossy in a bowl,'" Gram answered. Devin had been telling her about the diner slang Mrs. Costa used. Even though Gram hadn't heard it in years, she quickly got the hang of it again.

"Great!" Devin said. "Where's Mom?"

"Mom said not to wait for her for supper tonight. She's staying at the diner to mix up the batter for the chocolate cake."

Later that evening, Devin told Gram that he was going to the diner to visit Mom.

"Good idea," said Gram. "Take her some supper. She must be hungry by now."

"Here, Mom," Devin said as he walked into the diner. "I brought you some 'bossy in a bowl.'"

"Some what?" Mom asked. Then she looked at the container Devin was carrying. "Oh," she laughed. "Beef stew. Yum!"

"Are you almost finished mixing the cakes?" Devin asked.

"No such luck," said Mom. "I'll be up for a while yet, but I'll need to go to bed early tomorrow night so I can get up early Saturday to bake and frost. Do you think twenty cakes will be enough?"

"Sounds like plenty to me," said Devin. "Danny and I will go the park tomorrow and decorate our booth." Devin could hardly wait.

13

The Booth

Early Friday morning, Devin and Danny biked to the park in the middle of town. Their backpacks were stuffed with packages of red, white, and blue crepe paper, scissors, and plenty of masking tape.

The park was usually quiet and restful, but today it was swarming. People who worked for the town were setting up wooden booths. Some of the booths that had already been set up were being decorated by the people who would use them for selling things.

Devin looked around until he saw a table. Above it was a sign that said, "Booth Assignments Here."

"Look, there's the sign-in table," Devin said. "Hey, Mrs. Wallace is there." It was Mrs. Wallace's husband who had called the police the night Devin finally caught Squeezie. He had been walking his old dog past the diner just as Devin lunged at Squeezie. The light Devin had turned on and the noises from falling pots and pans made Mr. Wallace think that a burglar had broken in.

"Hi, Mrs. Wallace," Devin said when they got to the table.

"Good morning, Devin and Danny," said Mrs. Wallace. "What can I do for you today?"

"We need to find our booth," said Devin.

"Really? What will you be selling?" Mrs. Wallace asked with a smile. "Baby pythons?"

Devin smiled back. By now he had been teased about Squeezie by almost everyone in town. He didn't mind. In fact, it made him feel kind of special, especially since he had caught Squeezie and everything had turned out OK.

"Nope," he said, "chocolate cake and ice cream."

"Well, let's see," said Mrs. Wallace as she looked at a chart. "Booth 21 is yours. Booth 20 is selling lobster rolls and Booth 22 is selling crafts. So there won't be another dessert for miles."

Mrs. Wallace made some squiggles on an official sign-up sheet. "Good luck, boys!" she said as she handed it to Devin.

"Thanks, Mrs. Wallace," said Devin. "We'll save you a piece of cake!"

Devin and Danny found the booth and got busy. They hung red, white, and blue crepe paper from one side of the booth to the other. Before long, the booth looked ready for the festival.

The Booth

The two boys sat on the grass and studied their decorating. "The booth looks great," Danny pronounced. "It just needs a little something extra to make it different from the other booths. Something to make it really outstanding."

"Something besides a sign, you mean?" asked Devin.

"Yeah," said Danny. "I don't know what, though. Maybe we'll think of something later."

The boys sat in silence for a few minutes. Then Devin said, "Hey, Danny, I've been wanting to ask you something. Remember that time at the pier when you told me that I was fishing in your spot?"

"Yeah?" said Danny. He waited for Devin to go on.

Devin had thought that Danny might be embarrassed at being reminded that he had been mean. But he didn't seem embarrassed at all.

"Well, it just seemed like you were being really mean," said Devin.

"Really?" Danny sounded surprised. "That was the third fishing spot I had picked. Two other kids told *me* I was fishing in *their* spots. Now that I'd finally found a place that wasn't already taken, I wasn't about to give it up!" he said.

So Gram had been right, Devin thought. She had said that that was how they did things around here.

People found their fishing spots, and they hung on to them. He realized that Danny hadn't really been mean—just brave to stand up for what was his.

"I'd never be brave enough to tell someone that they were in my spot," Devin said.

"Sure you would," said Danny. "When something matters to you a lot, you'll stand up for it."

After a few minutes Danny said, "Now I know why you seemed so unfriendly when you asked me if I'd lost something. You thought I was mean!"

Devin smiled. "That's funny. You thought I was unfriendly, and I thought you were mean. It just goes to show how wrong people can be." Then he said, "If you thought I was unfriendly, how come you finally talked to me?"

"Because you turned in my knife. You didn't know who dropped it, and you could have kept it. But you turned it in to Mr. Gomez. My dad gave me that knife, and I was really glad to get it back. I thought you weren't very friendly, but that you were probably OK. So I took a chance."

Devin laughed. Then he said, "Hey, we have a sign to make. And ten more quarts of ice cream to crank out. We'd better get going!"

The Booth

At 8:00 that night, Devin's Mom got home from the diner.

"Finished!" she said to Devin and Gram. "I've mixed enough batter for twenty cakes. All I have to do is get up early to bake and frost them. Let's see. I figure that I can bake eight at a time in the big oven at the diner and two at a time in the oven here. That's ten cakes. They'll take forty minutes to bake, so twenty cakes will take about an hour and a half. By the time the second batch is done, the first batch will be cool enough to frost. Add two hours to frost the cakes . . ."

Mom decided to set her alarm for 5:30 A.M.

"Get me up, too, will you, Mom? I'll help you frost," said Devin.

"Thanks, sport," said Mom as she kissed him on the top of his head. "I'll wake you up when the first batch is cool—about seven. Now I'm going to take a shower and go to bed. The account book can wait until tomorrow. Goodnight, all!"

After Mom was out of hearing, Devin said to Gram, "I'm glad you'll be there to help us out tomorrow, Gram. We'll need a hand with scooping ice cream."

"With everybody at the festival, it should be a slow day at the diner," Gram said, "so I don't mind leaving your mom alone for a few hours. She'll be so surprised when she goes to the festival after she closes the diner," Gram went on, "and finds out that you're scooping homemade ice cream on top of her homemade chocolate cake!"

"Yup!" said Devin. "I hope the ice cream isn't gone by then. She hasn't even tasted it yet, and it's going to be a long time before I crank out another batch."

"Why is that?" asked Gram.

"Because my arm is too sore!" moaned Devin.

14

A Big Hit

Devin woke up the next morning and looked at his alarm clock. 8:00! Mom was supposed to wake him at seven! What happened? Didn't her alarm go off?

Devin ran to Mom's bedroom. Nope, Mom wasn't there. He dressed as fast as he could and ran to the diner. Mom was pouring a cup of decaf for a customer. But Devin didn't see any cakes.

"Good morning, honey," Mom said when she saw Devin. "Bad news. I got up to preheat the oven to bake the cakes, but the oven wouldn't work. No gas. So I called the gas company. They told me they got a report of a gas leak during the night. They had to turn off the gas to the diner until they can get it fixed. I guess I'll have to get by with the microwave today.

"Sorry, Dev," she went on. "I know it's disappointing, but we won't be able to sell cake at the festival. I was going to wake you up and tell them soon. Will you call Danny and Mrs. Costa to let them know? Or do you want me to tell them?"

Devin didn't say anything.

"Why are you grinning?" his mom asked. "You sure don't look disappointed!"

"Mom," Devin said, "just come to Booth 21 after you close the diner today. Promise?" Then he ran off to talk to Gram.

Later that morning, Mrs. Costa and Danny arrived to take Devin and Gram to the festival. Both Devin and Danny were wearing knickers and kneesocks with long-sleeved white shirts. At the last minute they decided to wear ties, too, because that's how Devin's great-grandpa was dressed in the photograph Gram showed them.

Gram was wearing her mother's long black dress with the white collar. On the collar was an old pin that Mom had bought at a yard sale. Devin was amazed at how much it made her look like her mother in the photo. And he couldn't resist pointing out to Gram that the cane she was using made her look *really* old-fashioned. Their attire certainly added to the old-fashioned feeling of their desserts.

Mrs. Costa got out of the car to show off her dress,

which she had bought at a store in town that sold old clothes. It was short and the waist came down to her hips. With it she wore three or four long necklaces. She had wrapped a purple scarf around her head to hold back her short hair. It contrasted nicely with the lavender color of the dress.

"What do you think of this?" she asked, twirling around for Devin and Gram.

"It's lovely!" Gram said. "It reminds me of pictures I've seen of my mother when she was young."

They had almost arrived at the park when Devin had a sudden thought. "Wait a second, Mrs. Costa!" he said. "I forgot the ice-cream maker! We have to go back to your house."

So Mrs. Costa turned the car around and drove back to her house. Devin ran inside and came out carrying the old-fashioned ice-cream maker.

When they arrived at their booth, they were surprised to see several other people there. A young man and woman were arranging dried flowers and wreaths on the counter and walls of the booth that Devin and Danny had decorated the day before. A little girl was helping them.

"What happened?" Danny asked Devin. "Did we decorate the wrong booth yesterday?"

"I don't know," answered Devin. He took out the

official piece of paper with the number of their booth written on it. Booth 21, it said.

Devin didn't know what to do. Was the booth they had decorated yesterday really number 21? Could he and Danny *both* have read the number wrong?

Devin started to panic. He needed to find Mrs. Wallace and hope that she could straighten things out. Or he needed to get Gram or Mrs. Costa to ask these people what they were doing there. Or perhaps he should—

Devin stopped and took a deep breath. Calm down, he told himself. You're thinking yourself into a box again. Just find out the number of the booth. Then go from there.

So Devin walked up to the young man and woman who were arranging the booth.

"Excuse me," he said. "Can you tell me the number of this booth?"

"It's number 21," the woman said, lifting the red crepe paper that Devin and Danny had used to cover the booth. There it was in big black numerals—number 21.

"Then this is *our* booth," said Devin. "See?" Devin showed them the official form with his name and Mrs. Wallace's squiggles next to his and Danny's name.

"But we have one of those, too," said the man. He pulled out a form with his name and the same booth number on it.

"Mrs. Wallace must have made a mistake," said Devin. "We spent all yesterday afternoon decorating this booth."

"Oh, really?" said the woman. "We thought that the festival committee had done this."

"Sorry," the man said to Devin. "We'll just take our stuff down."

Just then a big person in a lobster suit walked up. A lobster hood covered his whole head except for his eyes and mouth, and he was wearing a big button that said OFFICIAL LOBSTER.

"Is there something I can help you with?" the lobster asked. Devin recognized Mr. Wallace's voice.

The man explained the problem. Mr. Wallace apologized for the mix-up and offered to take the family to his wife, who he promised would straighten everything out.

"Thanks, Mr. Wallace!" Devin called out as he and the family walked away. Then he turned to Danny and said, "Mrs. Wallace must have forgotten to put our names on her chart. She was pretty busy."

"Yup," said Danny, smiling.

"Why are you grinning?" asked Devin.

"See?" said Danny. "A booth is like a fishing spot—once it's yours, you have to fight for it."

Devin laughed as he put the ice-cream maker where people could see it. "Now let's put up our sign," he said.

But first they had to change it. Devin took a big black marker and neatly crossed out the words "CHOCOLATE CAKE AND." Now the sign just said, "HOMEMADE VANILLA ICE CREAM FROM GRAM'S DINER."

Then Devin said to Danny, "I thought about what you said about the booth needing something to make it stand out. Here's what I came up with." Out of his back-pack he pulled the stuffed python Mom had given him.

"As long as Gram's is famous for having a python on the loose, we might as well take advantage of it!" he said.

"Devin! What on earth . . . !"

Mom had just arrived at the festival. All morning she had wondered why Devin insisted that she come to the booth when there was no cake to sell. Now she knew.

Mom read the sign aloud: "Homemade Vanilla Ice Cream from Gram's Diner." Then she laughed at the

CHOCOLATE CAKE
AND
HOMEMADE VANILLA
ICE CREAM
FROM GRAM'S DINER

stuffed toy python. Devin and Danny had wound it around one of the posts that held up the roof of the booth. They had attached a spoon with a big clump of yellow plastic on it to the python's tail and arranged the tail so that it was near its mouth. It looked like the python was about to eat a big spoonful of vanilla ice cream.

"Where in the world did you get the ice cream?" she asked.

"We made it, Mom!" Devin said. Scooping ice cream at the same time, he told Mom about the ice-cream maker he and Danny had found in the attic and the recipe they had found in Gram's cookbook and the days they spent making ice cream. He finished by saying, "It would be better if we had cake to go with it, but people seem to like it anyway!"

They sure did. People were buying dishes of ice cream as fast as Devin and Gram could fill them. Mrs. Costa was in charge of taking money and making change, and when he wasn't scooping ice cream, Danny was clearing away empty dishes and refilling containers of plastic spoons.

Devin and Mom saw Mr. Gomez walking toward them. He was carrying a dish of ice cream.

"Molly," he said, "this is my third dish of ice cream. It's delicious! This stuff is the real McCoy.

I didn't know you served homemade ice cream at the diner."

"Well, I don't," she said. "But thanks to Devin and his friends, it looks like I'm going to!"

Looking up at his mom, Devin could see how pleased she was at how the day had turned out, and how proud she was of him.

At last, he thought, I've done something right!

15

Sold Out!

"**O**h no!" said Mrs. Costa. "We're going have to close the booth early. We're running out of ice cream!"

Devin checked. "Yup," he said, "we only have three quarts left. At this rate we'll be sold out in fifteen minutes. And the festival doesn't close for two more hours!"

Mom and Mrs. Costa quickly made a sign.

SOLD OUT!
Coming Soon to Gram's Diner
HOMEMADE ICE CREAM

When the last dish of ice cream was sold, they hung the sign over the booth.

Sold Out!

"Let's clean up and go home," said Gram. "We've got things to do!"

"I'm starved!" Devin said when they got back to the diner. "The only thing I've had since breakfast is a dish of ice cream. Can we eat supper before we do anything else?"

"Sure!" said Mom. "Just hold on a minute, partner, and I'll rustle us up some grub."

"Now, you just sit!" Mrs. Costa ordered Mom. "You've done your share of cooking today. All I've done is make change. I'll get supper—just point me toward the kitchen. Is the gas working yet?"

It was, and Mom was glad for a break from cooking.

Before long, Mrs. Costa was putting steaming plates of hot dogs and beans in front of Gram, Devin, Mom, and Danny.

" 'Hounds on an island,' " said Gram. "My favorite Saturday night supper!"

"I'll bet you want some 'black moo' with that," Mrs. Costa said to Danny. "How about you, Devin? Do you want some chocolate milk, too?"

"Sure do!" said Devin.

All during supper, Devin kept looking at the metal box that held the money they made at the festival that day. How much was in it? No one mentioned the box, but Devin could tell that everyone else was curious, too.

After he and Danny cleared the supper dishes, Devin said, "The moment of truth has arrived. Let's count the money!"

First they put the twenty, ten, five, and one-dollar bills in separate piles. Then they put the half-dollars, quarters, dimes, nickels, and pennies in separate stacks. And finally they counted. Just to be sure, they counted again. And to make absolutely certain that there was no mistake, they counted a third time.

When they finished, they looked up at each other. "Wow!" they all said at once.

After she did the account book that night, Devin's mom called his dad. They talked for a while, and then she turned the phone over to Devin. Mom and Gram smiled as they watched Devin. They could tell how much his dad's words of praise meant to him.

Sold Out!

Before he and Dad ended the conversation, Devin said, "And Dad, Mom and Gram and I think it would be a good idea to buy an electric ice-cream maker. That way we could have plenty of homemade ice cream at the diner. We could even make different flavors! What do you think?" Devin smiled as he listened to Dad's answer. Then he and Dad said good-bye.

"Dad thinks it's a great idea to start serving homemade ice cream," Devin reported. "He said he'd shop around for an ice-cream maker in New York. Maybe he can find a used one that wouldn't cost much."

Mom smiled. "From the way things went at the festival today, selling homemade ice cream can't do anything but help. Even after we replenished your piggybank and gave Danny and Mrs. Costa their share, we made a nice little profit!"

"Mom," said Devin, "remember when Mr. Gomez said that our ice cream was the real McCoy? What does that mean? I always thought it was just something our family said when we answered the phone."

"It means that something is genuine, honey—the real thing. It was nice of Mr. Gomez to say that. I'm not sure where it comes from—something about a prizefighter, I think. We'll look it up at the library."

Mom yawned and stretched. "I'm going to bed now, sport. You should think about turning in, too. We've got a lot to do tomorrow."

"Tomorrow?" asked Devin. "Tomorrow's Sunday, Mom, and the diner's closed."

"I know," answered Mom. "But don't forget—we've got some cakes to bake and frost!"

Gram laughed. "It's a good thing we've got a big freezer," she said. "I've got a feeling that we're going to sell less cake in one day than we did ice cream!"

16

Kid McCoy

On Monday morning, Devin was sitting on the steps of the library, waiting for Miss Carson.

"Aren't you the early bird!" Miss Carson said as she climbed the steps with her key ring in her hand.

"Yup!" said Devin. "I'm a man on a mission. I need to find out where the phrase 'The Real McCoy' comes from."

Miss Carson's keys jingled as she opened the door. "You've come to the right place," she said. "We have an excellent dictionary of slang expressions."

Miss Carson set her purse and her bottle of water on her desk. Then she went to a shelf and took down a book.

"I think this will help you, Devin," she smiled.

Devin thumbed through the R pages. There it was—"real McCoy. See McCoy, the real," it said. Devin turned the pages to the M's. Finally he found what he was looking for.

The book said that in the late 1800s it was common for prizefighters to call themselves by the names of fighters who were more famous than they were. It got so that one fighter named Kid McCoy had so many imitators that he took to calling himself Kid "The Real" McCoy.

That's it! thought Devin. That other stuff they sell is just imitation ice cream. But ours is the real McCoy!

"Thanks, Miss Carson," Devin said as he handed her the book.

"Glad you found what you were looking for,

Devin," she answered. "By the way, you make great ice cream!" she called as Devin bolted out the door.

It took Devin's dad a couple of weeks, but he finally found a used ice-cream maker. Not long after that, it was up and running at Gram's Diner.

One afternoon on the way to the pier, Devin said to Danny, "It's a good thing Gram's ankle is finally healing. She's still got the cast on, but at least she can walk around without it hurting. Mom's really glad Gram can help dish out ice cream! She says that a lot of lunch customers are having ice cream for dessert now, and lots of people stop by in the middle of the day just for a dish of ice cream."

"It's great that your mom has made us official consultants," Danny said. "It's fun coming up with different flavors of ice cream!"

"Yeah!" said Devin. "Like your idea for chocolate ice cream with peanuts and chunks of peanut-butter cups. That's my favorite!"

"So, does it look like your family might be moving up here in the fall?" asked Danny.

Devin's cheerful face turned serious. "Well, it's still

too soon to say," he answered. "Business at the diner is a little better, but . . ." his voice trailed off.

"We can still hope," said Danny.

Devin's grin returned. "Yup!" he said.

17

Bad News

A few nights later, Mom got a call from Dad after Devin had gone to bed. They talked for a long time. Devin couldn't hear what they were saying, but for some reason he thought of the long talk Mom and Dad had the night Gram called to tell them about her broken ankle. He fell asleep thinking about how much his life had changed because of that talk.

The next morning Gram came into the kitchen as Devin was eating some shredded wheat cereal.

"That looks good," she said. "I think I'll have some 'baled hay' myself. Pass the 'moo,' please."

Devin passed Gram the milk. Between Gram and Mrs. Costa, he had gotten so used to diner lingo that it was like second nature to him.

"Your mom wants to talk to you after you've had breakfast," Gram said casually, without looking up from her bowl of cereal.

Devin knew that something was about to happen.

And he didn't think he was going to like what it was.

After breakfast Devin went to the diner. A customer was just leaving, and Mom was clearing dishes off the counter. She looked tired, as if she hadn't slept much. She looked worried, too.

Mom gave Devin a hug. "Sit down a minute, sweetie," she said. "We need to talk."

Devin sat down at the counter. Suddenly his hands felt clammy.

"Dad called last night," Mom began. She hesitated. Devin nodded his head as if to say, "Go on, Mom."

"John has had an accident, honey. He got hit on the head by a ball during a game," she said.

Devin looked shocked. "Is he OK?" he asked.

Mom nodded. "Yes, sweetie. Don't worry; he's OK. But he's still in the hospital. He got hit pretty hard, and he was unconscious for a while, so the doctors want to watch him. He might be able to go home in a couple of days, and when he does, I'm going to want to be there with him for a while."

So the bad news was that John had been injured; the good news was that he was going to be OK.

But Devin knew that there was more bad news coming.

"I'm afraid we'll have to close the diner, honey," Mom said.

"But—but," said Devin, "why do we have to close the diner when business has picked up?"

"Gram's ankle is still healing, Devin, and she can't take care of the diner by herself," explained Mom. "Besides, even though your ice cream is bringing in more customers, it's too soon to tell how big a difference it will make. I don't want you to get your hopes up about staying."

"But we need to give it more time, Mom," pleaded Devin. "Couldn't we find someone to help Gram? And I could help, too!"

"Even if we could find someone, we'd have to pay them, sweetie," said Mom. "And we can't afford that."

"Maybe Mrs. Costa could help," said Devin. "She always says how much she liked working at the diner in Gloucester and how tired she is of knitting!"

"I could never ask Denise to work for nothing, Devin," said Mom.

Devin looked at his mom. She was right. She couldn't ask Mrs. Costa to work for nothing. But *he* could.

18

It's a Deal

When Devin walked into the diner the next day, his mom and Mrs. Costa were talking.

"But Molly," said Mrs. Costa, "I don't call tips *nothing*. I'll work for tips, and I'll probably make a lot more than I do knitting. Now, you go to New York and take care of John. Gram, Devin, Danny, and I will take care of the diner. We'll do just fine. By the time John is well again, you'll have a better idea of how the diner's doing, and you and your husband will have more to go on before you decide whether to move the family up to Maine or stay in New York."

Mom sighed in relief. It made perfect sense. She left the same day.

The next day was rainy, keeping Devin and Danny from fishing. They were playing cards at Gram's kitchen table, inventing flavors of ice cream at the same time. Just as Devin suggested lobster-flavored ice cream, which they would sell at next year's Lobster Festival, the doorbell rang. It was the mail carrier with a package for Gram.

Devin and Danny brought the package to the diner, where Gram was sitting at the counter, refilling napkin holders.

"Package for you, Gram!" Devin said.

"Really?" said Gram. "I didn't order anything! Let's see what it is."

Devin helped Gram open the package. It was a book. The name of it was *Great American Diners.* Inside the cover was a note that said,

Dear Gram,

It takes a long time to get a book out. Bet you'd forgotten about this one. Thanks for your help. I hope to drop by sometime for another helping of your delicious meatloaf and mashed potatoes! I've visited a lot of diners, and believe me, Gram's is one of the best!

The note was signed by Stan Renaldi, the author of the book.

"Well, I never," said Gram. "That's the fellow who stopped by to take pictures for a book he was writing about diners! So this is what came of it! Denise, come take a look at this!"

Mrs. Costa came out from the kitchen, and she, Devin, and Danny leaned over Gram's shoulder while Gram leafed through the book, looking for Gram's Diner. She found it in the section titled "Great Diners of the Northeast."

"Wow!" said Devin and Danny.

"Great picture!" Mrs. Costa said.

"Oh my! The old place never looked so good!" Gram agreed.

"Look at this, Gram!" Denise said. "The caption says, 'If you're within a hundred miles of Blue Harbor, Maine, don't pass up a visit to Gram's Diner on Main Street. It's the real McCoy.'"

"Just like our ice cream!" Devin said.

One day a few weeks later, Gram's phone rang. It was Mom. She was calling from New York to give Gram and Devin their daily update on John.

Devin and John spoke, too. John sounded fine,

but Devin wondered if he thought he had let the team down by getting hurt. Devin knew how awful it felt to have let someone down.

Devin spoke with Mom again. After they had hung up, he told Gram, "Mom says that John's well enough to be alone for awhile, so she's driving up to Maine to visit. She says she'll be here on Monday. I can hardly wait to show her our surprise!"

"Me, too!" said Gram.

19

The Real McCoy

Monday morning was sparkling and beautiful, but Devin and Danny didn't go fishing. Instead, Devin sat on the front porch waiting for Mom, while Danny waited at the diner.

It was mid-morning when Mom's car finally drove into the driveway.

"Hi, Mom!" Devin yelled as he raced to give her a hug. He was shocked when Dad and John got out of the car, too.

"Hey, sport," Dad said, giving him a bear hug. "I sure have missed you!"

"My turn," said Mom.

"Whoa, look at you!" John said as he hugged Devin. "You're almost as tall as I am!"

The Real McCoy

"Look at *you*, you mean!" said Devin. "Does that still hurt?" He was talking about the bruise on John's forehead where he had been hit by the ball.

John gingerly touched the bruise. "Pretty ugly, isn't it? No, it doesn't hurt much anymore. The doc says it'll be there for a while yet, though."

"Have you been taking good care of Gram? Where is she?" Mom asked.

"She's at the diner. I told her I'd bring you over as soon as you got here. Let's go!" Devin said as he herded his family toward the diner.

As soon as they got inside, Mom came to a sudden stop. "I don't believe it!" she said.

The diner was almost full. Danny sat at the counter, eating a doughnut. Mrs. Costa was at the grill, cooking. Gram was behind the counter with her back to the door. She had just written down a customer's order for scrambled eggs and an English muffin. As she posted the order where Mrs. Costa could see it, she yelled,

" 'Wreck a pair and burn the British'!" Then she reached for the coffee pot and said to the customer, "Do you want a 'cup of joe' with that?"

Then she saw Mom, Dad, and John and came out from behind the counter to give them a hug.

"Gram!" said Mom. "You didn't tell me you had your cast off! And why didn't you tell me how busy you were? I'd have come back sooner!"

"Well, you had enough to think about, and I didn't want to raise false hopes. But I've got to admit we could use your help!" said Gram.

Mrs. Costa smiled and waved. She was too busy cooking to talk.

"But what happened?" asked Mom. "Why so many customers?"

"It started with Devin's homemade ice cream," Gram said. "Then when Denise began working here, she and I started swapping diner lingo around the customers, just for fun. They loved it. Word got around, and more and more people began coming in. Now it seems like everyone in town speaks diner lingo!

"Then one day a reporter from the newspaper showed up. He'd heard about Devin and Danny's ice cream and wanted to write a little story about it. Devin showed him the book on diners that I told you finally arrived. So the reporter wrote a story about the ice cream *and* the book, which brought in more customers. Then the Portland paper picked up the story, and—oops, gotta go," she said. "Here's another customer."

Before she left, Gram said, "There's just one problem. We keep running out of ice cream before we run out of customers!"

Gram went back behind the counter to get the customer's order.

"Give me a stack of 'blowout patches,' Gram," he said. "And bring me some 'Vermont' with it, please."

"See what I mean?" Gram said to Mom as she wrote down the order for pancakes with maple syrup.

Devin brought his family over and introduced them to Danny.

"So this is your partner in crime!" said Dad as he shook Danny's hand and beamed a smile at him.

Mom and John sat at the counter beside Danny. Mom said, "That doughnut is making me hungry!"

"There are plenty of 'life preservers' left," Danny answered.

Mom laughed. "I'm hungrier than that!"

Mom picked up the menu and began reading it. Devin watched her face closely to get her reaction. The menu was quite different from what it was when Mom left. It seemed that customers who came to eat in an old-fashioned diner wanted to eat old-fashioned diner food. That meant dishes like meatloaf, pot roast, liver and onions, fried chicken, fried clams, and something called a "blue plate special," which was whatever dish Gram and Denise decided to serve at a lower-than-usual price that day.

"We kept your salmon with cinnamon sauce, Mom," Devin said. "We took it off the menu for a few days to make room for steak, but people missed it!"

Mom laughed. She looked pleased to hear it.

"I think I'll have a western omelette with French fries," she said to Dev.

Devin turned to Gram and said, "Gram, Mom wants a 'cowboy with spurs'!"

"Make that two," John called out.

"Coming up!" said Gram.

Devin looked for his dad to ask if he wanted something to eat. But Dad wasn't paying attention. He was looking around the diner. He had one hand in his pocket, and he was scratching the back of his neck with the little finger of his other hand. Devin knew what that meant—his dad was deep in thought.

When the diner closed that day, Mom and Dad would be asking Gram to show them the account book. They'd probably be up late tonight going over the figures and talking about whether the diner was making enough to support the family.

How would it work out? Devin couldn't tell. Where would he be going to school a few weeks from now—here or in New York? He didn't know that, either. But it didn't really matter. What did matter was that for once he felt that instead of making things worse, he had helped make things better. If the diner worked out, he knew it would be partly because of him.

And it mattered that he had made a friend. Devin could hardly wait to tell Mom and Dad his and Danny's latest great idea. See, they could add a separate ice cream stand next to the diner. That would give them room to sell lots more flavors of ice cream—and milkshakes and sodas as well as sundaes with homemade toppings, too—which he and Danny would taste-test, of course.

Devin and Danny had already designed a sign to put above the ice-cream stand. Later he would show a sketch of it to Mom, Dad, and John. The sketch showed a big, happy-looking python holding an ice-cream cone in its tail and licking the cone with its forked tongue. Right now, the space above the python was empty. Devin would write the name of the ice-cream stand there, but he hadn't thought of one yet.

If Mom and Dad made up their minds quickly, they could have the ice-cream stand built by winter. By next summer, it would be in full swing. It should bring in lots of customers. Why wouldn't it? Like Gram's Diner, their ice cream was the real thing.

All of a sudden Devin knew what name he would write in the empty space on his and Danny's sketch.

The Real McCoy.